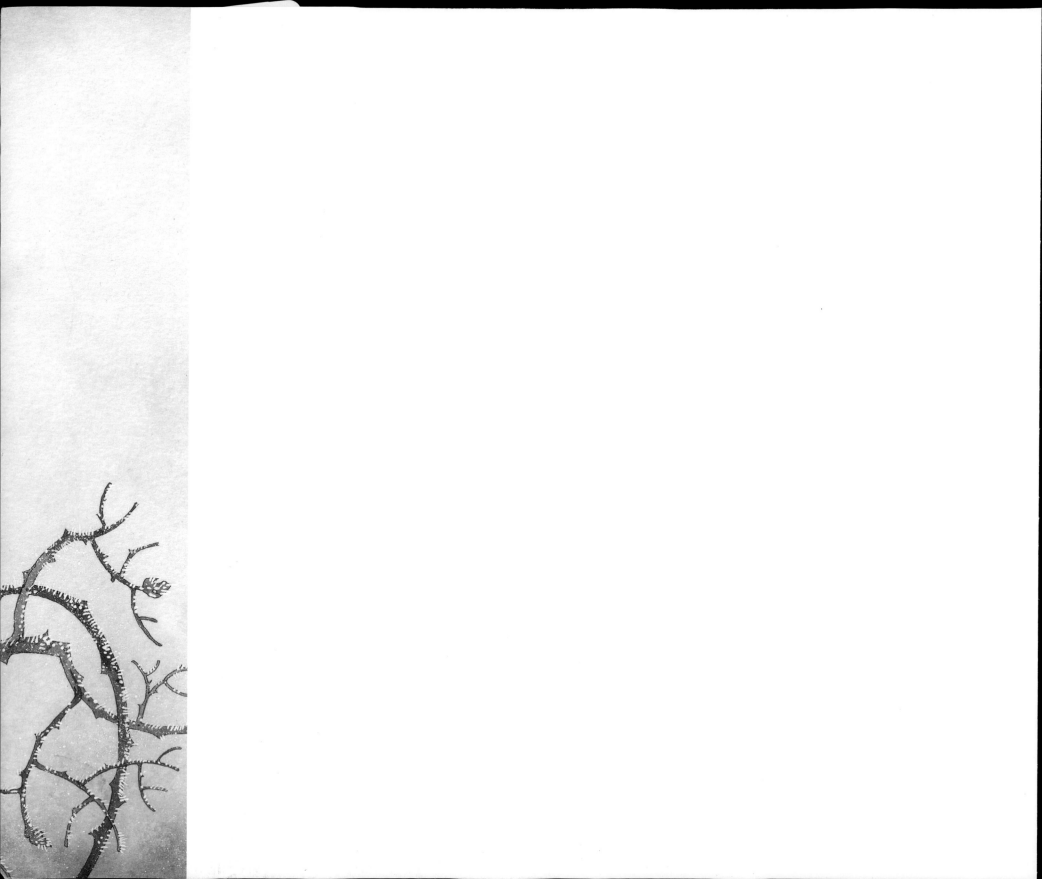

The
Town
Mouse
and the
Country
Mouse

For the mouse who knows
his own mind

First U.S. edition 2012

Library of Congress Cataloging-in-Publication Data is available.
Library of Congress Catalog Card Number pending
ISBN 978-0-7636-6098-7

12 13 14 15 16 17 18 TLF 10 9 8 7 6 5 4 3 2 1

Printed in Dongguan, Guangdong, China

This book was typeset in Bernard MT.
The illustrations were done in watercolor.

Edited by A. J. Wood

Templar Books
an imprint of Candlewick Press
99 Dover Street
Somerville, Massachusetts 02144
www.candlewick.com

The
Town
Mouse
and the
Country
Mouse

An Aesop Fable
retold &
illustrated by

Helen Ward

templar books
an imprint of Candlewick Press

There was once
a country mouse.

He lived a quiet life
among the seasons.

He knew the
insect-filled fields of
summer and the rich,
ripe orchards
of autumn.

He knew the aching hunger
of a long, cold winter
and the smell of the
sun-warmed earth
in the spring.

The country mouse knew
he was content.

Then, one spring morning,
his cousin arrived for a visit . . .
a fine, sleek city mouse
with a lot to say.

"In the city,
we don't have mud," he said.

"And we don't have
dangerous wild animals."

"In the city, we dine on rich, exotic foods in sumptuous surroundings."

"We have such amazing
sights and sounds—
noise and bustle and hum.
You should come
visit and see the
wonders of my city."

After his cousin returned
to the city,
the country mouse
grew less certain
of his contentedness.

He felt a longing for
new sights and sounds.

At the first chill
of winter, he hitched a ride
toward the bustle and hum
of the city.

The country mouse gazed up
at the high horizon where
the cold sky met
great towers of smooth
stone and glass.

The wonders of the
electric city crowded
his ears and eyes.

He discovered lights
in the dark
and automatic
ups and downs.

He found his cousin's
luxurious apartment.
And after exploring
the finery, he
settled in to
sleep.

But suddenly his
room was turned
upside down!

As he hid,
the country mouse recalled
his own grassy nest, all snug
and safe.

But then some sweet smells and his own grumbling stomach drew him to a feast just as delicious as his cousin had said.

A magnificent spread . . .

but also dangerous!

As they ran,
the country mouse
remembered with fondness
his own simple but quiet meals.

He also remembered
the song of the
thrush, the sound of a
worm in the earth,
and the buzz of crickets
in the hay meadows.

He longed
to be back beneath
a night sky
lit only by stars,
to be safe, to
be content . . .

to be home.

And once he was home,
he slept deeply.

Just a country mouse
dreaming of spring.

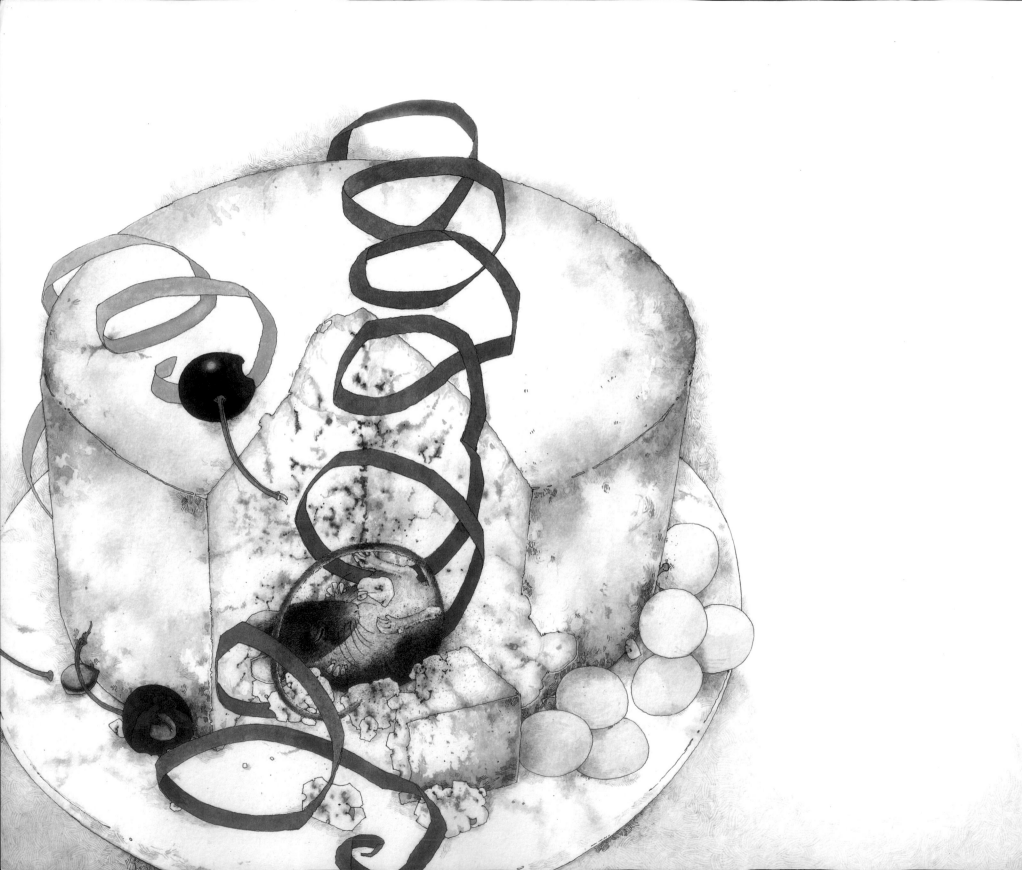